North
West
East
Towards South
South
You

My
Book of Shadows

Private Keep OUT!

This Spell Book belongs to:

____

CONTENTS

Moon Phases

Witch Facts

3 Spells

Pages for 13 more spells

Your Inspiration thoughts

Plenty of pages for you to write notes in.

The Witches Altar

Witches Tool Kit

Tool Chant, Witches Oath

The Five elements

To the New Witch

A Witches Health

2018 Diary

And MY SPELLS

Some Witch Facts:

- A Witch can be female or male
- Wichelen = To bewitch or forecast
- Wiccan = Pagan Witchcraft
- Witchcraft = Practice of Magic, either alone or in a group (coven)
- There are Good Witches, Winnie G
- There are Bad Witches, Winnie B
- There are White, Black, Red, Blue and Green magic
- Then there is the witchcraft of Winnie G. This is witchcraft for the young. Aha ha ha ha

Inspirational Thoughts

Write down some of your thoughts on the subjects below. Your thoughts create your magical beginning and bring you to the infinite universe as one and as a Witch.

Past:

Present:

Future:

Word Search: Find the Hidden word.
Hint: "Witches must xxxxx in themselves"

B E L I M E V W E K N N M E G
Z K M F C A I M E R T E M Q I
J K Y M L N G I N F K V F U L
K L K N N M M I A H C O M A I
M G K I F O H R C E A C R L A
B A E H O R C Y T T L M C I T
Y G R R C H E I J P B H W T Y
R D B G C T H E N P A N R Y X
P Z V T A W I V D N H S N M L
G N I L B T R W T O R P Q T N
Y W Q M T R N J K T M E L V H
P Z Q M K V P E T C K L T Y D
M M L O V E R M P B X L L T G
K R E D W G K T T Y F S R R M
Z W R A T L A X B E I N N I W

The word list

Ailig	Magic
Altar	Pentagram
Black	Red
Broomie	Spells
Chant	White
Coven	WinnieB
Equality	WinnieG
Freedom	Witch
Love	Witchcraft

My Book of Shadows

In this book of witchcraft,
I make my spells
Spells that tell
Do you smell them?
Can you?
Each potion that I create
Your senses they vacate
Until the magic is no mistake!
My spells are mine
And can only be cast by me
Nobody else will be able to cast my
spell...only me...Ahahaha.

Magic spells have been passed down by generations upon generations. In these pages of my book of shadows, I will write my spells, spells that I will create myself. I will use my imagination and research what is only good for me or good for others and add them to my spells. I will draw and write whatever I desire, for true and pure white magic is when one is free to write and draw with any creativity and without correction. Most of all, I will have loads of fun doing so. For I believe in myself.

Winnie G has given you three white magic spells and to begin your own book of shadows.

You are a good witch, your spells are only for good, and you will only cast good spells. If someone is being hurtful to you, then cast a good spell against their evil. And not against them. Remember, you will always be better than those that are evil towards you or others.

White magic is the purest form of magic that exists. It comes from the universe and rests in your heart. Use your magic to better yourself and the world around you. Live in freedom, peace and equality and you will grow to be the Good Witch.

Spell 1: To stop Nightmares

Spell 2: Getting rid of teenager spots or any spots on your face.

Bonus Spell 16: Requires a bit more effort and craft tools. But you can always put your guardians under a 'help me' spell.

Spells (Chants): Should always be said aloud, once.

The Witches Oath of Honour:

Take the witches oath before reading any further. You can say this oath once or whenever your believe wanders, but once said you live by it forever.

I'm a good witch

Past, present and future

My spells are cast

For good and protection

I love this universe

Everyone is one

We are all one

We live in peace, freedom and equality

No one that's good will come to harm with my spells.

I'm a good witch

The Witches Altar

Witches can have an altar, this is where you keep all your witchcraft items and cast your spells. You could have a Box as your portable altar, and keep all your magic tools inside. Or you could have a shelf in your room, where you place all your witchcraft items. Remember foods that can go off, should be stored in a fridge and discarded when due date has reached. All good witches make sure their health comes first and they do their magic in safety. Your witchcraft candles should never be left burning when no one is in the room, always have an adult present. You can always use Dream or LED Candles these do not have real flames, but will still carry the magic of the candle and are Winnie G witchcraft approved.

Candle Chant:

As the smoke rises, so does life's surprises

Your light, smell, touch and the air you breathe

Returns to the universe, For all that once was... Still is.

The starter
Witchcraft altar/kit:

A box (To put all your witchcraft items in. Do not put your candle in this box, it must always stay free and in the open unless you are travelling. But first, make sure it has been extinguished for at least one hour☺ or better still use a Dream or LED Candle, they are safer and still have magic)

Pencils

Paper

Envelopes

Chocolate

Bananas

Imagination

A tablecloth (Or paper with a pentagram drawn on it and laid down to represent a small tablecloth)

Candle (Use safely, ask an adult or use a LED candle)

Magic Wand (Can be a piece of stick)

Pentagram (You can draw this on a piece of paper, there are some at the end of the Book, either tear out or make copies of the page. Better still make your own.)

Book of Shadows (That's this book)

Most of the items you can make yourself, that way you can save some money for a rainy day. There are items you can purchase if you want, but you don't have to do so to be a witch.

Before you Begin any Magic spells...

Use this chant to send Magic to all your Witchcraft tools, you only need do this once. Then all your tools will contain the magic. If you get new tools, then you must cast this chant to fill them with magic.

The magic Tool Chant

Said while holding or looking at the items. Remember, your tools of magic are your friends, they are your tools of Magic. You must say this chant to all new tools or new food items that sit on your altar before they are used for the first time.

The Magic Tool Chant:

My Friends,

You cannot see

You cannot hear

You cannot smell

Everything on our earth can breathe, even stones can breath

You come from the universe

I ask you humbly to breathe my magic chant into your being

You are alive with magical powers

I thank you, my friends, for the power that you now provide me with

Witches never harm an animal or any other living creature to make spells no matter how small the creature is.

Witches cast spells from the goodness of their hearts to help others and themselves.

To the New Witch:

Spells sometimes do not work as you had planned. Don't worry it is not your fault! So why did my spell not work? Ok, everything that IS... Is part of the infinite universe. As such sometimes the universe will decide what magic it can allow. Sometimes the spell may not be in the best interest of everyone. Sometimes, we can get caught up in our own world, and what we want. But what we want sometimes is not enough, sometimes others that are involved need to want it as well. But always remember to cast your spells with your full believe and your best intentions, so don't worry if your spell did not work. You can always try again, sometimes a change to a spell will do a power of good. For example, you have spots, the spot spell did not work. But did you take care? Have you been washing your face regularly with unscented and pure soap?

Spells do not replace common sense. Spells work in conjunction with everything else that needs to be in place first. Spells give you the power to believe in yourself. Before you can love another, you must love yourself. Spells cannot force another to do what you want, but they can help you achieve what is good for you. And if the universe wishes it to be the same... then it will be so.

Spells are cast to help others, and that includes our natural world. Witches never harm animals or our natural environment. A witch never uses the blood of anything for their spells. A true witch is at one with themselves and the universe around us all.

Create your spells and cast them well. But remember have loads of fun, and always enjoy what you do. And only create good spells.

Spell ideas can come from research.

Research what is good for you and the universe.

You can read books, online and by sitting quietly in a room.

Five minutes of meditation per day will help your imagination go a long way.

You have 13 spells that you can create yourself in your book of shadows plus the three that Winnie G gave you, that's 16 spells of witchcraft. Think what you want your spell to do. Help someone? Empower yourself? Find happiness? And many of the other ideas that come into your imagination. There is no hurry to create spells, take your time and enjoy.

The book of shadows is your personal journey, your personal thoughts, it's your diary of your life. Its pages will eventually contain your feelings, happiness, sadness, sweat, aspirations, hopes and pain. This book is your roadmap throughout your life's journey, so enjoy.

The Five elements:

Fire

Earth

Air

Water

Yourself. You are the lifeform element.

These five elements are the energies that surround us and are part of your witchcraft. The elements are part of your universe.

The pentagram represents the five elements.

The circle that you will draw on the ground around you. (Or you can place a pentagram on the ground around where you will cast your spells. If there is more than one witch, then each of you will stand within the circle of pentagram's that you place on the floor around you.)

The circle helps to contain your witchcraft, the magic energy and to keep evil forces at bay.

Your pentagram points north, west, east and south (South has 2 points, this is represented by SOUTH and YOU. (See the Witches Pentagram below.) The True south point as per a compass is the middle point between 'south' and 'you' pointing in the opposite direction from north.

Each point represents an element. Sometimes witches use the following colours of a candle to represent the elements. Candles can be placed on your floor to represent this. (Only use Led dream or led candles — do not use 'lit' candles. Lit candles should be used with care and with an adult present)

North (Earth) (Green Candle)
South (Fire) (Red Candle)
West (Water) (Blue Candle)
East (Air) (Yellow Candle)

The Fifth Element (YOU): You are the spiritual energy. Your colour is that of a rainbow and your shape is that of a star. You are 'one' with the universe and the universe is 'one' with all that exists.

Notes

The Witches pentagram

A witch's health:

Witches look after their health when doing their witchcraft by:

Wash your hands before and after handling food

When using food items for consumption, make sure you store it correctly

Never eat any food items that are 'off' or past the due by date

Never eat food items that you are allergic to. Example. If you are allergic to chocolate then you must not eat it or use it. In these instances, you will replace the spell ingredients by using another item that is OK for you to eat or be near.

Candles, I recommend Dream or LED candles, these do not require to be lit, and they still contain all the magic of other types of candles. However, if you are using candles that you light with a flame, then you must make sure, that an adult supervises you.

Never be alone with any open flames.
Keep all your witchcraft items away
from young children or anything that
is flammable.

Keep all of your witchcraft items
together either in your witchcraft
box or your altar.

Notes:

Notes:

Notes:

About Witchcraft Kits

If you are **a teenager** you can use LED candles or candles that you can light (of course it may still be subject to a responsible adults consent?)

If you are **not a teenager**, then you should definitely use a LED candle, they are safer and less Messy. And your witchcraft will be just as great.

The Witchcraft kit that you will need is sorted in order of what you require for spell 1 and 2. The other items will help you make further spells. As your ideas and spells grow so will the tools that you will require.

1 - Magic Wand (can be any piece of stick)

2 - Chalk for making your circle

3 - Pencil

4 - White pentagram paper (you can use plain paper and draw your own pentagram on it - Your book of shadows contains 10 pieces of pentagram paper that you can gently tear or cut from this book and use for your spells)

5 - Chocolate bar (dark or milk)

6 - Candle (preferably a LED candle. IMPORTANT: If you use a candle that needs to be lit, then you must ensure a responsible adult is with you at all times!)

7 - Banana (s)

8 - **Book of Shadows** (That's this book)

9 - **Pentagram altar cloth** (Or one piece of pentagram paper laid down to represent a cloth. It does not matter if it only covers a small area of the table. You can invest in a cloth at a later time if you want)

10 - **Imagination, lots of it**

11 - **Box or altar, to put all your witchcraft items in.** [Altar can be a shelf or table in your room. Never put a hot candle into a box or cupboard. Your box can be plain or you can decorate it with anything that your heart desires.]

All of the above is for Spell 1 and 2. Below is the bonus spell.

12 – (4 x Herbs) Introduction (Get from any supermarket)

Fennell (**Good for** aiding digestions. **Use to** keep curses away. **How to use**, eat a tiny bit raw, or mix in with any potion. It tastes a little like liquorice before and after casting your spell)

Garlic (**Good for** digestion, hair and skin. **Use for** magical healing for your inner body. **How to use**, eat a tiny amount before and after you cast your spell. You can mix it in your potions as well. Don't rub your eyes after use...they will sting)

Ginger (**Good for** travel sickness or any sickness. **Use for** relaxation or after a large meal. **How to use**, each a tiny bit before and after casting your spell or mix it with a potion)

Jasmine (**Good for** nerves. **Use for** attracting Love or money. **How to use** make a small drink with it and sip before and after casting your spell)

13 -   A   pentagram   pendant (optional)

14 - Essential Oil [not for eating]

15 - 3 Crystals (Optional)

16 - Unscented Potpourri or it can be a mixture of flowers, leafs and petals [not for eating]

17 - Mixing Bowl

Notes

Notes:

Where to purchase your witchcraft items:

Some Witchcraft items can be purchased at Winnie G's witchcraft shop. Or you can buy them at any other store. Some items you may have in your home already. Some items you can create and make yourself. You don't need to spend a lot of money on your witchcraft supplies. Make do with what you have.

Notes:

Notes

Spell 1:
<u>To Stop Nightmare's</u>

Are you having nightmares? Then the nightmare spell will remove or reduce their power over you. Letting you sleep with ease and being at one with your dreams.

<u>Tools needed:</u>

Pencil (not pen)

Paper (white)

An envelope (colour and size do not matter) If you don't have an envelope fold it inside another piece of paper.

Chocolate (dark or milk)

The Magic spell (The Chant)

The Spell (Chant once)

Happy Face, I desire

Sad Face, covered in chocolate

Scary Face covered in chocolate

Sad and Scary Face is no longer my nightmare

Happy Face is my desire

I cast this spell, and my nightmares shall no longer scare me

What to do:

1. - On the piece of paper, draw a happy face and immediately next to it draw a sad face. Underneath both faces draw a scary face.

2. - Get your chocolate and lick your finger, rub your wet finger on the

chocolate until you have some chocolate melted onto your finger.

3 - Rub your chocolate finger on the sad and scary face.

4 - While holding the paper in your hand. (You must look at the paper while saying your spell. Now, cast your spell, you must do it with belief

5 - Fold the paper up and place it into the envelope

6 - Place the envelope under your pillow before you go to sleep.

If your nightmares return in the future, repeat all of your steps and cast your spell again.

My personal Notes re Spell 1:

Spell 2:
Get rid of spots

Are you fed up with spots, or acne as it is called? Well, these are a natural occurrence as your body changes. No spell can remove these, for to do so, would mean having to change the future evolution of everyone on earth.

But... casting a spell will help make them disappear and carry on their work hidden from prying faces. But remember all witches should eat healthily. You must believe in what you are doing or the magic will not work.

Tools Required:

Piece of white paper

Pencil (not pen)

A small banana still in its skin (or half
a large banana – keep the other half
for tomorrow night's spell)
An envelope (colour and size do not
matter) If you don't have an
envelope fold it inside another piece
of paper.
The Magic Spell (Chant Once)

The Spell (Chant Once)

My face! My face!

What has my youth done to me?

Spots are good to me

My spots I love

My spots will heal

I cast this spell on my spots to bother
me no more

<u>**What to do**</u>

1 - Do these steps at least 1 hour before you go to bed for your night's rest.

2 - Take the paper and draw two faces on it

3 - On one of the faces draw as many spots as you think you have

4 - On the other face, draw a happy face with two small spots.

5 - Now, peel the banana and eat all of the banana.

6 - Take one piece of the banana skin and rub it on the paper face with all the spots that you pencilled.

7 - Take the remaining banana skin and rub the inside of the skin onto the spots on your own face. Rub

it all over every spot that you have.

8 - Now, take your spell and chant with belief and meaning 3 times.

10 - Fold the paper with the faces and position into the envelope. Just before you go to bed place the envelope under your pillow.

11 - Do this every night for the first week. Then at least twice a week thereafter or until your happy.

Remember your spots may fade or they may remain. If they remain, continue to rub a fresh banana skin on those pesky spots and eat ½ a banana daily (remembering to say your chant.) If they still remain, then they are not ready to

leave you yet. But you are ready to love
and accept them.

My personal Notes re Spell 2:

Spell 3:

Spell 4:

Spell 5:

Spell 6:

Spell 7:

Spell 8:

Spell 9:

Spell 10:

Spell 11:

Spell 12:

Spell 12 and 12/13ths

There is no spell 13, that's because the 13th spell is reserved for the highest of the witches, Winnie G. She is the only one that can cast a 13th spell, without it turning into Bad Magic. Bad magic is what Winnie B uses. JUST DON'T DO IT!

Spell 14:

Spell 15:

BONUS Spell 16
<u>To lift Sadness</u>

Just for you my male and female witches!

This is a quick spell for when you feel sad. And we witches are like anyone else we can get sad too!

You can use this to cast a spell to help your family, friends and yourself.

You will need:

A few drops of 'Ylang Ylang' Essential Oil, a bag of Potpourri (a bowl full), a Lepidolite

Chrystal, a **mixing bowl** and a **bowl** to put your potion mixture into.

How to: Put your potpourri into the mixing bowl, then add the crystal, then add 5 drops of essential oils. Mix it all together with your hands while saying your spell. Once mixed and spell said, take out the Chrystal and hold it in your hand. Clean the Chrystal and put it back on your altar or box. Rub your hands together, so you are rubbing the oil into your skin.

The Spell (Chant)

With this spell I cast

The air is stale
I don't want my spell to fail
We are sad
Yet we are far from bad

The air we now breathe is fresh
This new aroma surrounds our flesh

Sadness is one of our emotions that
reside in our hearts
But for a while, I need you to
DEPART
Please leave sadness
So we can be filled with happiness

What you need to do: To cast the sadness spell: Always remember to have done the new tool chant (if you have not already done so)

1 - Put your pentagram paper down on the table or altar.

2 - Mix your ingredients and Chrystal [remember to say your spell as you mix]

3 - Take out the Chrystal (Lepidolite**), hold it in your hand. Next, clean the Chrystal with your hands and put back on your altar. Your hands will now be filled with the magic potion.

4 - Take the bowl and leave it in the room where everyone visits.

Say your spell in every room your bowl stands.

5 - Remember to speak in a positive manner when talking to anyone in that room. Because negative thoughts and talks will undo all that magic you have just created.

6 - In a day or two, and when the sweet aroma stops smelling, you can add a few drops of essential oil to the bowl, while saying you Sadness Spell. This will help your spell last a wee bit longer.

** *If you do not have a Lepidolite Chrystal, use another Chrystal and charge it with your tool chant.*

Spell 16 Notes:

5 pages for Notes, Drawings and Ideas

It's not the end, it's only the beginning. Now I will get another book to record more of my spells...Aha ha ha ha

North
West
East
Towards South
South
You

North
West
East
Towards South
South
You

North
West
East
Towards South
South
You

North
West
East
Towards South
South
You

North
West
East
Towards South
South
You

North
West
East
Towards South
South
You

North
West
East
Towards South
South
You

North
West
East
Towards South
South
You

North
West
East
Towards South
South
You

North
West
East
Towards South
South
You

North
West
East
South
Towards South
You

143

BE AWARE of...

Please note: Witchcraft and witches are a part of the fabric of our superstitions created throughout our history on earth.

This book is a fun youth's book, but it would not hurt an adult to practice the same rituals within.

What this book is not: This book is not a historical fact! Nor may it fully resemble other books of witchcraft.

This book is Winnie G's witchcraft.

The book does: Contain some known and documented items of original witchcraft. But the main theme is for the youth to have fun and in a safe environment.

Do not:

Participate in anything with people you do not know, regardless of the similarities or sympathy's that they may have or share with what you do. **And** always check with a responsible adult, even when not in any doubt. Because evil people go on holidays too!

Notes

Notes

Notes

Word Search: Find the Hidden Word'
Hint: "A witch will xxx the ingredients together"

```
M   I   L   L   A   X   S   R   N   G   N   T
X   P   K   K   G   P   S   I   H   T   V   C
H   A   V   E   E   R   K   T   X   A   B   G
W   N   L   L   V   R   H   D   O   H   Y   W
Y   W   L   N   Q   V   X   L   R   W   U   D
Y   R   E   V   E   A   L   S   H   O   D   O
M   E   W   Y   T   H   H   Y   Y   Z   M   O
A   J   H   M   C   L   X   M   O   W   D   G
G   K   V   T   V   M   J   K   I   U   C   D
I   R   I   R   S   R   D   T   X   R   R   D
C   W   Q   W   M   I   H   L   D   R   X   O
V   S   T   N   E   I   D   E   R   G   N   I
```

Word List

all	the
do	this
Good	to
have	what
ingredients	Witch
is	with
magic	you
Reveals	your
spell	

Register at:

https://www.jeanmegaw.com

To be kept up-to-date with her new releases and to become a registered Winnie G Witch.

Thank you for purchasing my book

Thanks To:
Izakowski, vgorbash, Ptkang and
prometeus
For providing the Photo Art.

This book is a work of fiction, Names, characters etc. are either a product of the author's imagination or are used fictitiously. Any resemblance to actual persons, living, dead or still to be born 'may or may not' be entirely coincidental.

Any reality is purely to demonstrate a real, current, and debatable feel to the story. All characters names in this book can be personalised by the publisher to create your own personal storybook.

No part of this book can be reproduced in any form, including but not limited to; written, electronic or mechanical, including photocopying, recording, or by any information retrieval system without the written permission from the publishing company.

The right of Jean Megaw to be identified as author of this work has been asserted by her in accordance

Published by Three Zombie Dogs® McLaughlin's Close, Derry, BT48 6SZ. All rights reserved. Copyright © 2017 Jean Megaw

A copy of this book has been deposited at The Legal Deposit Office, The British Library. ISBN: 978-1-912039-60-9

First Published by 3ZombieDogs 2017

North
West
East
Towards South
South
You

My 2018 Diary

Private and Personal

My Diary For 2018

Have fun with your diary, recording your daily rituals in writing was an old tradition since the beginning of time. Historical witches would have written on pieces of parchment with the ash from their old wands.

A diary is your personal experiences of your everyday life. It is your personal journey of your life. It will contain all that you write on its pages.

This diary is one page per week, but you will be amazed what you can write if you only jot down a few sentences each day. And when you look back on your diary it will remind you of your past.

Understanding your future is in understanding your past experiences.

The Diary has been left blank with only the dates entered. The moon phases will be different to where you live. You can always go to this cool website and find the moon phases for the area that you reside in.

You can enter those into your diary along with any local holidays and events.

You can even collect and stick some cool and colourful stickers in your diary from any resources that you can find. Witches have been known to collect leafs and then press them into their book of shadows.

For the moon phases near your home town go to:

https://www.timeanddate.com/moon/phases/

The Witches Moon

Despite landing on the moon, it will always be a mystery and as such the moon holds a magical power over everyone on earth. Witches try and harness the magic of the moon to cast the spells that they have created.

It is not only witches that try to harness the power of the moon. Many other civilisations and religions have used the moon in their ceremonies. Some misguided earthlings used the moon to sacrifice animals and humans in their quest for power to their gods.

A good witch will never-ever sacrifice an animal or person. A good witch will never spill a drop of blood making or casting their spells.

A good witch believes in equality.

There is a huge amount of folklore based on the subject of the moon.

One thing for certain is a witch will use the phases of the moon to cast their spells. During this time the moon can make you feel tired, happy, sad, overjoyed and at one with yourself.

Your emotions can sometimes get the better of you. Understanding how you feel will also help you make informed decisions on your personal life.

A witch's purpose is to save the earth, a witch will align themselves with the phases of the moon cycle. This is where a witch becomes one with themselves and earth.

The moon phases can help transform your life and it may surprise you to learn just how powerfully the moon affects us all and our planet.

Phases of the moon cycle	Moon Looks like this when you are facing the moon
Dark Moon	Invisible
Waxing Crescent	Slim crescent (right side)
1st Quarter	half full (right side)
Waxing Gibbous	3/4 full (right side)
Full Moon	full, round
Waning Gibbous	3/4 full (left side)
3rd Quarter	half full (left side)
Waning Crescent	Slim crescent (left side)

Holidays and Observances for Ireland

1 Jan	New Year's Day	Lá Caille
17 Mar	St. Patrick's Day	Lá Fhéile Pádraig
19 Mar	<u>St. Patrick's Day observed</u>	Lá Fhéile Pádraig
30 Mar	Good Friday	Aoine an Chéasta
1 Apr	Easter	Domhnach Cásca
2 Apr	Easter Monday	Luan Cásca
7 May	May Day	Lá Bealtaine
4 Jun	June Bank Holiday	Lá Saoire Bainc (Meitheamh)
6 Aug	August Bank Holiday	Lá Saoire Bainc (Lúnasa)
29 Oct	October Bank Holiday	Lá Saoire Bainc (Deireadh Fómhair)
24 Dec	Christmas Eve	Oíche Nollag
25 Dec	Christmas Day	Lá Nollag
26 Dec	St. Stephen's Day	Lá Fhéile Stiofáin
31 Dec	New Year's Eve	Oíche Chinn Bliana

2018 Moon Phases Calendar

Jan   2:○,   8:◑, 17:●, 24:◐, 31:○

Feb   7:◐, 15:●, 23:◑

Mar   2:○,   9:◐, 17:●, 24:◑, 31:○

Apr   8:◐, 16:●, 22:◑, 30:○

May   8:◐, 15:●, 22:◑, 29:○

Jun   6:◐, 13:●, 20:◑, 28:○

Jul   6:◑, 13:●, 19:◐, 27:○

Aug   4:◑, 11:●, 18:◐, 26:○

Sep   3:◑,   9:●, 17:◐, 25:○

Oct   2:◑,   9:●, 16:◐, 24:○, 31:◑

Nov   7:●, 15:◐, 23:○, 30:◑

Dec   7:●, 15:◐, 22:○, 29:◑

The above are the moon phases for the City of Derry in Northern Ireland. You can always get your moon phases for your city by going to www.timeanddate.com

Monday, January 1, 2018

Tuesday, January 2, 2018

Wednesday, January 3, 2018

Thursday, January 4, 2018

Friday, January 5, 2018

Saturday, January 6, 2018	Sunday, January 7, 2018

| Monday, January 8, 2018 |
| Tuesday, January 9, 2018 |
| Wednesday, January 10, 2018 |
| Thursday, January 11, 2018 |
| Friday, January 12, 2018 |

Saturday, January 13, 2018	Sunday, January 14, 2018

Monday, January 15, 2018

Tuesday, January 16, 2018

Wednesday, January 17, 2018

Thursday, January 18, 2018

Friday, January 19, 2018

Saturday, January 20, 2018	Sunday, January 21, 2018

| Monday, January 22, 2018 |
| Tuesday, January 23, 2018 |
| Wednesday, January 24, 2018 |
| Thursday, January 25, 2018 |
| Friday, January 26, 2018 |

| Saturday, January 27, 2018 | Sunday, January 28, 2018 |

Monday, January 29, 2018

| Tuesday, January 30, 2018 |

| Wednesday, January 31, 2018 |

| Thursday, February 1, 2018 |

| Friday, February 2, 2018 |

| Saturday, February 3, 2018 | Sunday, February 4, 2018 |

Monday, February 5, 2018

Tuesday, February 6, 2018

Wednesday, February 7, 2018

Thursday, February 8, 2018

Friday, February 9, 2018

Saturday, February 10, 2018	Sunday, February 11, 2018

Monday, February 12, 2018

Tuesday, February 13, 2018

Wednesday, February 14, 2018

Thursday, February 15, 2018

Friday, February 16, 2018

Saturday, February 17, 2018	Sunday, February 18, 2018

Monday, February 19, 2018
Tuesday, February 20, 2018
Wednesday, February 21, 2018
Thursday, February 22, 2018
Friday, February 23, 2018

Saturday, February 24, 2018	Sunday, February 25, 2018

Monday, February 26, 2018

Tuesday, February 27, 2018

Wednesday, February 28, 2018

Thursday, March 1, 2018

Friday, March 2, 2018

Saturday, March 3, 2018	Sunday, March 4, 2018

Monday, March 5, 2018

Tuesday, March 6, 2018

Wednesday, March 7, 2018

Thursday, March 8, 2018

Friday, March 9, 2018

Saturday, March 10, 2018

Sunday, March 11, 2018

| Monday, March 12, 2018 |
| Tuesday, March 13, 2018 |
| Wednesday, March 14, 2018 |
| Thursday, March 15, 2018 |
| Friday, March 16, 2018 |

| Saturday, March 17, 2018 | Sunday, March 18, 2018 |
| | |

Monday, March 19, 2018

Tuesday, March 20, 2018

Wednesday, March 21, 2018

Thursday, March 22, 2018

Friday, March 23, 2018

Saturday, March 24, 2018	Sunday, March 25, 2018

Monday, March 26, 2018

Tuesday, March 27, 2018

Wednesday, March 28, 2018

Thursday, March 29, 2018

Friday, March 30, 2018

Saturday, March 31, 2018

Sunday, April 1, 2018

Monday, April 2, 2018

Tuesday, April 3, 2018

Wednesday, April 4, 2018

Thursday, April 5, 2018

Friday, April 6, 2018

Saturday, April 7, 2018	Sunday, April 8, 2018

Monday, April 9, 2018
Tuesday, April 10, 2018
Wednesday, April 11, 2018
Thursday, April 12, 2018
Friday, April 13, 2018

Saturday, April 14, 2018	Sunday, April 15, 2018

Monday, April 16, 2018

Tuesday, April 17, 2018

Wednesday, April 18, 2018

Thursday, April 19, 2018

Friday, April 20, 2018

Saturday, April 21, 2018

Sunday, April 22, 2018

| Monday, April 23, 2018 |

| Tuesday, April 24, 2018 |

| Wednesday, April 25, 2018 |

| Thursday, April 26, 2018 |

| Friday, April 27, 2018 |

| Saturday, April 28, 2018 | Sunday, April 29, 2018 |

| Monday, April 30, 2018 |
| Tuesday, May 1, 2018 |
| Wednesday, May 2, 2018 |
| Thursday, May 3, 2018 |
| Friday, May 4, 2018 |

| Saturday, May 5, 2018 | Sunday, May 6, 2018 |

| Monday, May 7, 2018 |
| Tuesday, May 8, 2018 |
| Wednesday, May 9, 2018 |
| Thursday, May 10, 2018 |
| Friday, May 11, 2018 |

Saturday, May 12, 2018	Sunday, May 13, 2018

Monday, May 14, 2018

Tuesday, May 15, 2018

Wednesday, May 16, 2018

Thursday, May 17, 2018

Friday, May 18, 2018

Saturday, May 19, 2018	Sunday, May 20, 2018

Monday, May 21, 2018

Tuesday, May 22, 2018

Wednesday, May 23, 2018

Thursday, May 24, 2018

Friday, May 25, 2018

Saturday, May 26, 2018	Sunday, May 27, 2018

Monday, May 28, 2018

Tuesday, May 29, 2018

Wednesday, May 30, 2018

Thursday, May 31, 2018

Friday, June 1, 2018

Saturday, June 2, 2018

Sunday, June 3, 2018

Monday, June 4, 2018	
Tuesday, June 5, 2018	
Wednesday, June 6, 2018	
Thursday, June 7, 2018	
Friday, June 8, 2018	
Saturday, June 9, 2018	Sunday, June 10, 2018

| Monday, June 11, 2018 |
| Tuesday, June 12, 2018 |
| Wednesday, June 13, 2018 |
| Thursday, June 14, 2018 |
| Friday, June 15, 2018 |

| Saturday, June 16, 2018 | Sunday, June 17, 2018 |

Monday, June 18, 2018

Tuesday, June 19, 2018

Wednesday, June 20, 2018

Thursday, June 21, 2018

Friday, June 22, 2018

Saturday, June 23, 2018	Sunday, June 24, 2018

| Monday, June 25, 2018 |
| Tuesday, June 26, 2018 |
| Wednesday, June 27, 2018 |
| Thursday, June 28, 2018 |
| Friday, June 29, 2018 |

| Saturday, June 30, 2018 | Sunday, July 1, 2018 |

Monday, July 2, 2018

Tuesday, July 3, 2018

Wednesday, July 4, 2018

Thursday, July 5, 2018

Friday, July 6, 2018

Saturday, July 7, 2018	Sunday, July 8, 2018

Monday, July 9, 2018
Tuesday, July 10, 2018
Wednesday, July 11, 2018
Thursday, July 12, 2018
Friday, July 13, 2018

Saturday, July 14, 2018	Sunday, July 15, 2018

Monday, July 16, 2018

Tuesday, July 17, 2018

Wednesday, July 18, 2018

Thursday, July 19, 2018

Friday, July 20, 2018

Saturday, July 21, 2018

Sunday, July 22, 2018

| Monday, July 23, 2018 |
| Tuesday, July 24, 2018 |
| Wednesday, July 25, 2018 |
| Thursday, July 26, 2018 |
| Friday, July 27, 2018 |

| Saturday, July 28, 2018 | Sunday, July 29, 2018 |

Monday, July 30, 2018

Tuesday, July 31, 2018

Wednesday, August 1, 2018

Thursday, August 2, 2018

Friday, August 3, 2018

Saturday, August 4, 2018	Sunday, August 5, 2018

Monday, August 6, 2018

Tuesday, August 7, 2018

Wednesday, August 8, 2018

Thursday, August 9, 2018

Friday, August 10, 2018

Saturday, August 11, 2018	Sunday, August 12, 2018

| Monday, August 13, 2018 |

| Tuesday, August 14, 2018 |

| Wednesday, August 15, 2018 |

| Thursday, August 16, 2018 |

| Friday, August 17, 2018 |

| Saturday, August 18, 2018 | Sunday, August 19, 2018 |

Monday, August 20, 2018

Tuesday, August 21, 2018

Wednesday, August 22, 2018

Thursday, August 23, 2018

Friday, August 24, 2018

Saturday, August 25, 2018	Sunday, August 26, 2018

| Monday, August 27, 2018 |
| Tuesday, August 28, 2018 |
| Wednesday, August 29, 2018 |
| Thursday, August 30, 2018 |
| Friday, August 31, 2018 |

| Saturday, September 1, 2018 | Sunday, September 2, 2018 |

| Monday, September 3, 2018 |
| Tuesday, September 4, 2018 |
| Wednesday, September 5, 2018 |
| Thursday, September 6, 2018 |
| Friday, September 7, 2018 |

| Saturday, September 8, 2018 | Sunday, September 9, 2018 |

Monday, September 10, 2018

Tuesday, September 11, 2018

Wednesday, September 12, 2018

Thursday, September 13, 2018

Friday, September 14, 2018

Saturday, September 15, 2018

Sunday, September 16, 2018

Monday, September 17, 2018

Tuesday, September 18, 2018

Wednesday, September 19, 2018

Thursday, September 20, 2018

Friday, September 21, 2018

Saturday, September 22, 2018	Sunday, September 23, 2018

| Monday, September 24, 2018 |
| Tuesday, September 25, 2018 |
| Wednesday, September 26, 2018 |
| Thursday, September 27, 2018 |
| Friday, September 28, 2018 |

| Saturday, September 29, 2018 | Sunday, September 30, 2018 |

| Monday, October 1, 2018 |
| Tuesday, October 2, 2018 |
| Wednesday, October 3, 2018 |
| Thursday, October 4, 2018 |
| Friday, October 5, 2018 |

| Saturday, October 6, 2018 | Sunday, October 7, 2018 |
| | |

Monday, October 8, 2018

Tuesday, October 9, 2018

Wednesday, October 10, 2018

Thursday, October 11, 2018

Friday, October 12, 2018

Saturday, October 13, 2018	Sunday, October 14, 2018

Monday, October 15, 2018

Tuesday, October 16, 2018

Wednesday, October 17, 2018

Thursday, October 18, 2018

Friday, October 19, 2018

Saturday, October 20, 2018	Sunday, October 21, 2018

Monday, October 22, 2018

Tuesday, October 23, 2018

Wednesday, October 24, 2018

Thursday, October 25, 2018

Friday, October 26, 2018

Saturday, October 27, 2018	Sunday, October 28, 2018

| Monday, October 29, 2018 |
| Tuesday, October 30, 2018 |
| Wednesday, October 31, 2018 |
| Thursday, November 1, 2018 |
| Friday, November 2, 2018 |

| Saturday, November 3, 2018 | Sunday, November 4, 2018 |

| Monday, November 5, 2018 |
| Tuesday, November 6, 2018 |
| Wednesday, November 7, 2018 |
| Thursday, November 8, 2018 |
| Friday, November 9, 2018 |

| Saturday, November 10, 2018 | Sunday, November 11, 2018 |

| Monday, November 12, 2018 |

| Tuesday, November 13, 2018 |

| Wednesday, November 14, 2018 |

| Thursday, November 15, 2018 |

| Friday, November 16, 2018 |

| Saturday, November 17, 2018 | Sunday, November 18, 2018 |

Monday, November 19, 2018

Tuesday, November 20, 2018

Wednesday, November 21, 2018

Thursday, November 22, 2018

Friday, November 23, 2018

Saturday, November 24, 2018	Sunday, November 25, 2018

Monday, November 26, 2018

Tuesday, November 27, 2018

Wednesday, November 28, 2018

Thursday, November 29, 2018

Friday, November 30, 2018

Saturday, December 1, 2018	Sunday, December 2, 2018

Remember to order your 2019 Book of Shadows Diary

| Monday, December 3, 2018 |
| Tuesday, December 4, 2018 |
| Wednesday, December 5, 2018 |
| Thursday, December 6, 2018 |
| Friday, December 7, 2018 |

Saturday, December 8, 2018	Sunday, December 9, 2018

| Monday, December 10, 2018 |
| Tuesday, December 11, 2018 |
| Wednesday, December 12, 2018 |
| Thursday, December 13, 2018 |
| Friday, December 14, 2018 |

Saturday, December 15, 2018	Sunday, December 16, 2018

Monday, December 17, 2018

Tuesday, December 18, 2018

Wednesday, December 19, 2018

Thursday, December 20, 2018

Friday, December 21, 2018

Saturday, December 22, 2018

Sunday, December 23, 2018

| Monday, December 24, 2018 |
| Tuesday, December 25, 2018 |
| Wednesday, December 26, 2018 |
| Thursday, December 27, 2018 |
| Friday, December 28, 2018 |

Saturday, December 29, 2018	Sunday, December 30, 2018

| Monday, December 31, 2018 |
| Tuesday, January 1, 2019 |
| Wednesday, January 2, 2019 |
| Thursday, January 3, 2019 |
| Friday, January 4, 2019 |

| Saturday, January 5, 2019 | Sunday, January 6, 2019 |

2017 Highlights

My Journey

Have loads of fun with your daily notes, it's something to look back on!

Time goes so quickly, you have just finished one year already.

Any notes that you have entered will give you an indication of your time on earth during 2017.

This book is your personal journey, your personal history on earth.

This book is now in the PAST

What is PRESENT is your individual moment in each precious second on earth.

Your FUTURE is being written with each thought and each pathway you choose.

Your PATHWAY is not written in stone, you can change or take a different path at any moment in your life.

REMEMBER, no pathway is the wrong pathway, each pathway will lead you on a journey. Sometimes that journey is the wrong one, don't agonise, and simply take a new and better pathway.

Notes

Notes